Hope Larson • Brittney Williams • Sarah Stern

GOLDIE VANCE™

Volume Two

BOOM! BOX™

GOLDIE

BOOM! BOX™

GOLDIE VANCE Volume Two, May 2017. Published by BOOM! Box, a division of Boom Entertainment, Inc.

A catalog record of this book is available from OCLC and from the BOOM! Studios website, www.boom-studios.com, on the Librarians page.

BOOM! Studios, 5670 Wilshire Boulevard, Suite 450, Los Angeles, CA 90036-5679. Printed in China. First Printing.

ISBN: 978-1-60886-974-9, eISBN: 978-1-61398-645-5

VANCE™

created by Hope Larson & Brittney Williams

written by
Hope Larson

illustrated by
Brittney Williams

colors by
Sarah Stern

letters by
Jim Campbell

cover by
Brittney Williams

designer
Jillian Crab

editors
Dafna Pleban & Shannon Watters

chapter FIVE

issue five cover by **Brittney Williams**

ST. PASCAL, FLORIDA.
5:45 AM.

Paff

HUFF

GASP

ZZZZZZ...
GOLDIE!

WH-WHA'S WRONG, CHERYL?!
WHEN I SAID GO AT YOUR OWN PACE, I DIDN'T MEAN GO TO SLEEP!

I WASN'T ASLEEP! I WAS--I WAS STRETCHING. GOTTA STAY LIMBER.
AT THIS RATE YOU'LL NEVER PASS THE PHYSICAL!

WE AREN'T ALL DESTINED TO BE ASTRONAUTS LIKE YOU.
I CAN'T BELIEVE YOU'D TRADE ALL OF OUTER SPACE FOR ANOTHER HOUR OF SLEEP! WHAT ABOUT SCIENCE? WHAT ABOUT THE MYSTERIES OF THE COSMOS?

WHAT ABOUT DRAG-RACING ON THE MOON?

MOON GRAVITY IS A SIXTH OF WHAT IT IS ON EARTH, SO I BET THERE'S ALL KINDS OF COOL TRICKS YOU COULD--
HEY, CHER? ARE YOU SURE YOU WOKE ME UP?

OR AM I DREAMING?
UNREAL!

WHAT DO WE DO?!

LET'S GET THE HELMET OFF. IT SHOULD *TWIST* LIKE--
POP

ST. PASCAL GENERAL HOSPITAL.
SHE'S WAKING UP, DOCTOR!
Ungh.
MY *HEAD*...

DON'T TRY TO MOVE. YOU'RE SEVERELY DEHYDRATED. LORD KNOWS WHAT YOU'VE BEEN THROUGH.
W-WHERE AM I?

YOU'RE IN ST. PASCAL, FLORIDA. YOU WASHED UP ON OUR BEACH.
CAN YOU TELL US WHO YOU ARE? YOU WEREN'T CARRYING I.D.

I CAN'T REMEMBER ANYTHING.

She looks so familiar, but I can't place her.
Was she a guest at the hotel?

I don't think--
WOULD YOU GIRLS EXCUSE YOURSELVES? WE NEED TO RUN SOME TESTS.

SHE'S NOT A GUEST. AND SHE'S NOT A REAL ASTRONAUT--AT LEAST, NOT ONE OF OURS.
Huh? HOW D'YOU KNOW?

AS YOU KNOW, I HAVE A SIGNED PHOTOGRAPH OF ASTRONAUT ALAN SHEPARD ON THE WALL NEXT TO MY BED.
IT'S THE FIRST THING I SEE IN THE MORNING AND THE LAST THING I SEE AT NIGHT.

THIS "ASTRONAUT'S" SPACE SUIT IS IDENTICAL TO HIS MERCURY IV SUIT, EXCEPT FOR ONE THING: THE NASA LOGO.

WHAT'S WRONG WITH IT? I DIDN'T NOTICE.
OF COURSE YOU DIDN'T--BECAUSE IT'S NOT THERE AT ALL.

EXCUSE ME--

ARE YOU THE GIRLS WHO FOUND THE ASTRONAUT?
YES! ARE YOU FROM THE PAPER? ARE WE GONNA MAKE THE FRONT PAGE?!

WE'RE NOT FROM THE PAPER. WE'RE FROM NASA.
-Hurk-

UH, WELL, SORRY YOU GASSED OUT HERE. THE WOMAN IN THERE--SHE'S NOT ONE OF YOURS.
HER SUIT'S IDENTICAL TO A MERCURY IV, BUT YOUR LOGO ISN'T ON IT ANYWHERE.
...

YOU MUST BE A GREAT FAN IF YOU CAN RECOGNIZE A MERCURY IV.
WHAT'S YOUR NAME, DEAR?

...
GOLDIE, *uh,* VANCE. AND THAT'S MY FRIEND CHERYL.

WELL, GOLDIE U. H. VANCE, HERE'S MY CARD. WE'RE ACTIVELY RECRUITING TEENS LIKE YOU FOR THE *LOVELACE YOUTH IN SPACE PROGRAM.*
I'LL TELL MY ASSISTANT WE'RE EXPECTING YOUR CALL.

THANKS...

THAT WAS WEIRD.

HEY, WHAT--?!
?!

WHAT'S WRONG?!

IT WAS SUPPOSED TO BE ME, GOLDIE! ME! NOT YOU!
WHAT? YOU MEAN THE LOVELACE THING?

I'M SMART, I'M ATHLETIC, I KNOW EVERYTHING ABOUT SPACE--I'M EVEN 5'10", THE IDEAL ASTRONAUT HEIGHT--
HOW WERE THEY SUPPOSED TO KNOW? YOU WERE ALL CLAMMED UP!

GOOD THING I SAID SOMETHING, OR WE WOULDN'T HAVE THIS.
TAKE IT, OKAY?

NO. THEY DON'T WANT ME.
COME ON. THIS IS A DUMB MISUNDERSTANDING. IT'S NO BIG DEAL.

NO BIG DEAL?

YOU'RE RIGHT. WHO CARES ABOUT MY LIFELONG DREAM?
THAT'S NOT WHAT I--

HEY!
ARE YOU 5'10" WITH OR WITHOUT THAT HIGH HORSE YOU'RE RIDING?!

MEANWHILE, AT CROSSED PALMS RESORT...
WHAT DO YOU MEAN, THE BEACH IS CLOSED?!

IT'S JUST OUR BEACH WHICH IS CLOSED, MADAM. THERE ARE SEVERAL DELIGHTFUL PUBLIC BEACHES NEARBY.
BEACH
C'MON, GRAN. THAT SOUNDS FUN, DON'T IT?
I DIDN'T COME TO FLORIDA TO MIX WITH THE LOCAL RIFF-RAFF!

NOW, STEP ASIDE!
MADAM, YOU CANNOT--

WHAT--WHAT HAS HAPPENED HERE? WHAT VILE GOINGS-ON ARE YOU HIDING FROM YOUR GUESTS?

MURDER!
MADAM, PLEASE! THERE HAS BEEN NO SUCH THING. WE CAN'T EVEN SAY, YET, IF A CRIME HAS BEEN COMMITTED--
THERE'S BEEN A MURDER!
-GROAN-
WOW, DAD. I MISS ONE SHIFT AND THE PLACE FALLS APART.

I BOOKED MY STAY AT CROSSED PALMS, NOT CROSSBONES!
C'MON, MRS. CHESTER. LET'S FIND YOUR CAR AND GET YOU OUTTA MURDERVILLE.

GOODBYE!

AND GOOD RIDDANCE.

HEY, ROB? CAN YOU HOLD DOWN THE FORT? I WANNA CHECK IN WITH WALTER AND--

Oh.

GREEN CROSTON SEDAN!

PINK FLANSBY JUNIOR!

BLACK STEENO SPECIALE!

TWO HOURS LATER...
Whew, THAT'S THE LAST OF 'EM! AND CHERYL THINKS I WOULDN'T PASS A PHYSICAL--
INCOMING!

VRROOM

Oof! I MADE IT!
WELCOME TO THE CROSSED PALMS. CHECKING IN?
I--ah--oh, COME ON, I KNOW YOU'RE IN THERE.
AGENT LADNER. FEDERAL BUREAU OF INVESTIGATION. I'M LOOKING FOR DETECTIVE WALTER TOOEY.
FBI

HEY, NOSEBLEED!
LAYLA?!

I CAN'T BELIEVE THIS! HOW LONG'S IT BEEN?
Oh, HONEY! DON'T MAKE ME DO THE MATH.

WHAT ARE YOU DOING HERE?
Oh. I'M, uh...

YOU DIDN'T TELL ME YOU KNOW AN FBI AGENT.

HOT DEAL! YOU JOINED THE BUREAU?
COOL YOUR CHOPS, WALT. IT'S A LOTTA PAPERWORK, MOSTLY.
I BET IT'S LOADS MORE FUN TO BE THE DETECTIVE AT A CLASSY RESORT.

AGENT LADNER!
SORRY, KIDS. I'M NEEDED.

WELL, HEY--IF YOU NEED A PLACE TO DO PAPERWORK, I'M ON THE FIRST FLOOR, BY THE ELEVATORS.

LOOK AT YOU, WALT-- T.C.B.* WITH THE F.B.I.
YOU MOVED ON HER LIKE IT WAS NO BIG THING!
*Taking care of business.

MOVED ON IS RIGHT. AGES AGO. WE DATED IN HIGH SCHOOL.
WHO DUMPED WHO?

IT WASN'T LIKE THAT. SHE WAS A COUPLE YEARS AHEAD, SO WHEN SHE GRADUATED...
YOU DATED AN OLDER WOMAN?! gasp THIS STORY GETS BETTER AND BETTER!

Cough
SO YOU AND CHERYL FOUND THE GIRL, huh?
YEAH. ANY CLUE WHO SHE IS?

NOTHIN' TO HANG YOUR HAT ON.
CHERYL SAID SHE LOOKED FAMILIAR.

GUESS I BETTER FOLLOW UP. Sigh
I SURE HOPE SHE'S COOLED DOWN BY NOW.

CROSSED PALMS FRONT DESK.
Oh! HI, TREY. WHERE'S CHERYL?

THINGS TA DO. PLACES TA BE. SHE ASKED ME TO COVER.

Oh, I SEE. SHE ASKED YOU NOT TO TELL ME WHERE SHE WENT.
I'M NOT GETTING INVOLVED.

SHE ASKED YOU NOT TO TELL ME THAT SHE ASKED YOU NOT TO TELL ME WHERE SHE WENT.

BLINK ONCE FOR YES, TWO FOR NO.

YOU'RE A PIECE OF WORK, GOLDIE VANCE.

wink

Wax Lips RECORDS
IT'S SO DUMB, DIANE! HOW CAN I APOLOGIZE IF SHE'S AVOIDING ME?

I JUST WANNA FIX IT AND MOVE ON.
GOLDIE, YOU'RE GREAT AT FIXING THINGS.
BUT SOMETIMES I THINK YOU FIX THEM SO YOU DON'T HAVE TO THINK ABOUT HOW THEY GOT BROKEN.

MAYBE THAT'S WHAT CHERYL WANTS YOU TO DO.
BUT IT WAS AN ACCIDENT!

SEE, BABE? THAT'S THE THING. IT'S NOT AN APOLOGY IF YOU AREN'T SORRY. JUST... TRY TO PUT YOURSELF IN HER SHOES.
Ahem.

YOU DO BUY-BACKS?
YEAH. YOU WANNA SEE PETER.

COME ON THROUGH THE PEARLY GATES AND PREPARE TO BE JUDGED FOR YOUR SINS AGAINST MUSIC.
Urk.
~Sigh~
PUT MYSELF IN HER SHOES. OKAY.
OOH! I CAN'T WAIT TO PARK THAT BAD BOY!
OUTTA MY WAY!
CHERYL?! WHAT ARE YOU DOING HERE? YOU AREN'T A VALET!
SO? I CAN HANDLE IT. IT'S JUST A CAR.
JUST A CAR?! IT'S AN ELKO ELEKTRA A70!
COME ON, GOLDIE! IT'S NOOOO BIIIIG DEEEEEAL!
VRRRRRRR

VRRRRRR
OKAY, DIANE. YOU'RE RIGHT, AS USUAL.

ST. PASCAL GENERAL HOSPITAL.
IF I KNOW CHERYL, SHE'S BACK AT THE HOSPITAL, VISITING OUR ASTRONAUT.

Oh. SHE MUST'VE SWITCHED ROOMS.

ONLY-- WHAT'S THAT?

HER HOSPITAL I.D. BRACELET?
DOE, JANE.
ADMITTED: 08/11/62. SEX: F

Huh?!

VRRRRRRRRRRR
CHERYL?!

CHERYL DOESN'T HAVE A CAR!
CHERYL DOESN'T HAVE A DRIVER'S LICENSE!
AND WAS THAT THE ASTRONAUT?!
WHERE ARE YOU GOING, CHER?
AND WHAT HAVE YOU GOT YOURSELF INTO?

chapter

SIX

issue six cover by **Brittney Williams**

ST. PASCAL.
ANEMONE LANE.

W. Tooey

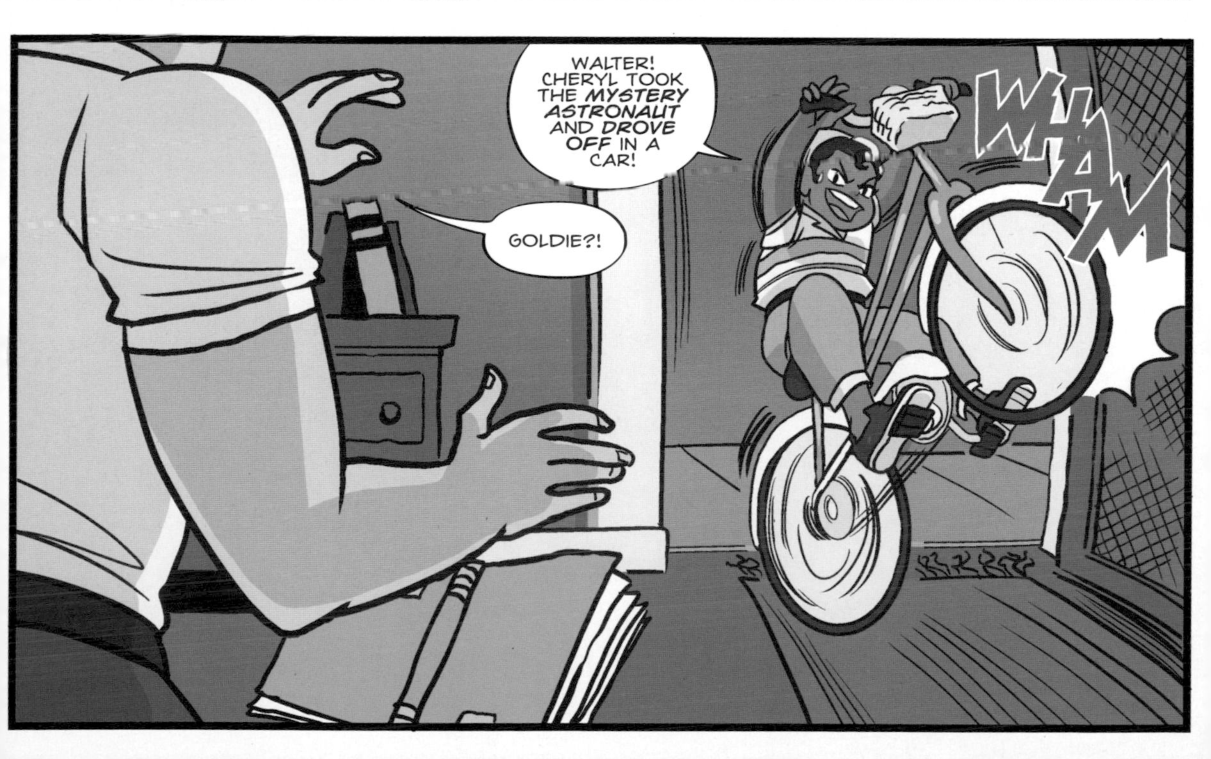
WALTER! CHERYL TOOK THE MYSTERY ASTRONAUT AND DROVE OFF IN A CAR!
WHAM
GOLDIE?!

WHO IS THIS SPACE-WOMAN? COULD BE THE RUSSIANS AGAIN.
OR SOMEONE WHO STAYED AT THE HOTEL. CHERYL SAID SHE LOOKED FAMILIAR.

BUT THE REAL MYSTERY IS, WHY WAS CHERYL DRIVING A CAR?!
SHE DOESN'T HAVE A LICENSE OR A SET OF WHEELS!

AT LEAST, NOT LAST I CHECKED...

WHY DON'T WE TALK TO HER BOYFRIEND? HE MIGHT KNOW SOMETHING.
ROB?

IT'S 8 P.M. THIS TIME OF DAY HE HANGS OUT AT THE DEEP END.

BUT CHER'S MY BEST FRIEND. WHAT WOULD SHE TELL ROB THAT SHE WOULDN'T TELL ME?
LET'S FIND OUT.

DEEP END DINER, 8:05 P.M.
DeepEnd
Uhhh, HOW'D YOU FIND OUT ABOUT CHER'S CAR?

YOU FIRST, ROB.

I, uh, TOOK HER TO THE D.M.V. FOR HER DRIVING TEST.

AAAAND I GAVE HER CAR THE ONCE-OVER BEFORE SHE BOUGHT IT. MADE SURE SHE GOT A GOOD DEAL.
Uh-huh.
THAT WAS A MONTH AGO.

SHE'S HAD WHEELS FOR A MONTH?! I CAN'T BELIEVE SHE DIDN'T TELL ME!

C'MON, GOLDIE. CAN YOU BLAME HER? YOU HAVE STICKY FINGERS WHERE CAR KEYS ARE CONCERNED.

EXCUSE ME, BUT--

BUT... YEAH, YOU GOT A POINT.

SHE COULDN'T HAVE YOU "BORROWING" HER CAR. SHE NEEDED IT FOR HER OTHER JOB.
A SECOND JOB? DOING WHAT?

I DUNNO. SHE SEEMED EMBARRASSED, SO I DIDN'T ASK.
PAGEANTS.

WHAT?

WHILE YOU WERE INTERROGATING ROB'S MILKSHAKE, I CALLED CHERYL'S HOUSE.
SHE'S NOT THERE, AND HER MOM SAID SHE HEADED DOWN TO BELLEPORT FOR A *BEAUTY PAGEANT* TOMORROW.

I'M DATING A *BEAUTY QUEEN?* WOW!
SHE'S BEEN COMPETING FOR MONTHS, SAVING HER PRIZE MONEY FOR COLLEGE.*
*ANNUAL TUITION FOR M.I.T., CHERYL'S DREAM SCHOOL, CIRCA 1963: $1500.

YOU OKAY, GOLDIE?
YEAH, JUST...
SHE HAS A WHOLE LIFE I DIDN'T KNOW ABOUT.

MAYBE THE ASTRONAUT BELONGED TO *THAT* WORLD. SHE DEFINITELY LOOKED LIKE A BEAUTY QUEEN.

WE'VE GOTTA GO TO BELLEPORT!

OR WE COULD TELL THE FBI AND LET *THEM* INVESTIGATE. DON'T WANNA STEP ON ANY TOES.

ESPECIALLY NOT WHEN THEY'RE ATTACHED TO ***AGENT LADNER,*** *hmm?*

LISTEN, WALT--BY NOW THE BUREAU KNOWS THAT ASTRONAUT'S MISSING. THEY'VE GOT THEIR ***OWN*** INVESTIGATION TO WORRY ABOUT.

IF WE VISIT OUR PAL AT HER EVENT AND JUST ***HAPPEN*** TO LEARN SOMETHING USEFUL, WHO COULD FAULT US?
AND I'LL BET AGENT LADNER WOULD BE IMPRESSED.

OKAY, BUT WE CAN'T JUST BARGE IN AND DEMAND ANSWERS. THOSE BELLEPORT GIRLS WON'T GIVE THE SHINE OFF A RHINESTONE TO SLOBS LIKE US.
Hmm. YOU'RE RIGHT.

I'VE GOTTA GO... ***UNDERCOVER.***

AND SO...
BEEP BEEEEP
DON'T WIG OUT, I'M COMING!

OUCH, DIANE! HAVEN'T YOU DONE THIS BEFORE?

JUST EVERY NIGHT FOR THE FIRST THREE YEARS OF HIGH SCHOOL.
YOU HAD LONG HAIR?

"YEP. BUT THE DAY OF THE SENIOR HOMECOMING DANCE, I SNAPPED AND CUT IT OFF.

"I FELT SO GLAMOROUS, LIKE AUDREY HEPBURN--BUT MY BOYFRIEND HATED IT. SAID I'D EMBARRASSED HIM."

I DUMPED HIM ON THE DANCE FLOOR, AND MY HAIR'S BEEN SHORT EVER SINCE.

siiiigh
YOU'RE SO COOL.
HOPE SO. I PAID MY DUES.
SO HAVE YOU THOUGHT ABOUT MAKEUP? LET'S SEE YOUR DRESS.

IT'S AN OLD ONE OF MY MOM'S.

FLOP
Ummm, GOLDIE...?

Oh NO! THAT'S ONE OF HER SPARE TAILS!* I--I MUST'VE GRABBED THE WRONG BAG.
DON'T WORRY. I BROUGHT A BACKUP.
*GOLDIE'S MOM, SYLVIE, WORKS AS A LIVE MERMAID AT ST. PASCAL'S MERMAID CLUB.

TA-DAAA!

IT'S LOVELY, DI, BUT THERE'S NO WAY IT'LL FIT.
WE'LL SEE.

BEACHY-KEEN MOTOR LODGE, 10 P.M.
Oh, FLASH! I TOLD YOU! THIS WHOLE PLAN'S A WASH OUT.

Shhh. DON'T SWEAT IT, GOLDIE. GET YOUR BEAUTY SLEEP AND LEAVE THE REST TO ME.

11 P.M.
2 A.M.
5 A.M.
z z Z...
7 A.M.
-gasp- DIANE!

THIS IS THE BEST DISGUISE EVER!

ALL I HAVE TO DO IS KEEP MY ANKLES FROM BREAKING...
WOBBLE

AND MY CURLS FROM UNCURLING...
WILT

AND MY FACE FROM SLIDING OFF.

THAT'S *MY* JOB.

YOU'RE THE RACE CAR. I'M THE MECHANIC.
VROOM!

BELLEPORT HALL.
GOOD LUCK, LADIES!
DRY CLEANING PAGEANT
WOBBLE

Dressing Room

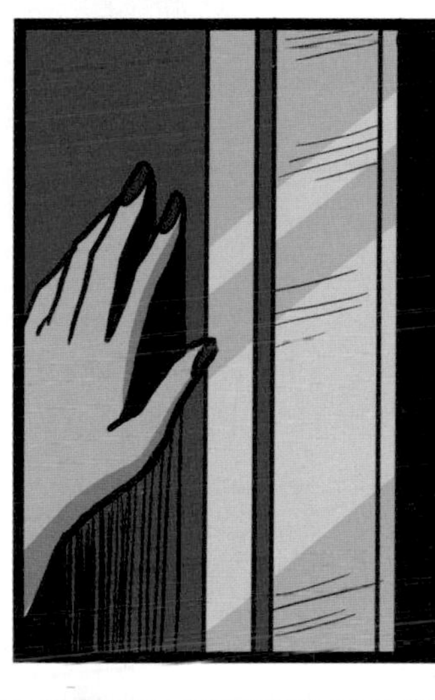

So much for blending--
HI!

IF YOU'RE LOOKING FOR THE FUTURE FLIGHT ATTENDANTS ASSOCIATION, THEY MEET ON **TUESDAYS.**

IS THAT WHAT I LOOK LIKE? A FLIGHT ATTENDANT?!
NO... THIS **IS** THE MISS **SPEE-DEE DRY CLEANING PAGEANT,** ISN'T IT?

...
CORRECT.

HERE GOES NOTHING.
Oh! WHAT A RELIEF! WHEN I SAW EVERYONE DRESSED **WRONG,** I GOT WORRIED.

DRESSED WRONG? **EXCUSE** ME?

GOLLY, DIDN'T **ANYONE** GET THE ADDENDUM?
THIS PAGEANT ISN'T ABOUT **UPHOLDING** THE STATUS QUO-- IT'S ABOUT SPEEDING **FORWARD** THROUGH TIME AND IMAGINING THE PAGEANTS OF THE **FUTURE!**

gasp

Eep!
THANK GOODNESS YOU SHOWED UP! NONE OF US WOULD'VE KNOWN!

YOU HEARD HER, GIRLS! WE STILL HAVE TIME TO REWORK OUR OUTFITS. THE PAST IS DEAD! THE FUTURE IS NOW!

rip!
tear!
Spritz!
Primp!

SAY, D'YOU KNOW IF CHERYL'S COMPETING? CHERYL LEBEAUX?

SHE CALLED IN SICK, AND THANK GOSH FOR THAT! THE REST OF US HAVE A SHOT, FOR ONCE.
DOES SHE WIN LOTS OF PAGEANTS?

FALL IN, ROOKIE. I'M GOING TO SHOW YOU SOMETHING.

THIS IS THE **HALL OF QUEENS.**
AFTER EACH PAGEANT, A PHOTO OF THE WINNER IS PLACED HERE.

AS YOU CAN SEE, CHERYL'S WON SIX OF THE LAST EIGHT EVENTS ON THE BELLEPORT CIRCUIT.
ATTA GIRL, CHER!

Huh?
THAT'S THE ASTRONAUT! IT'S **GOTTA** BE!

HEY, *um*, DID YOU KNOW HER?
MILLIE TEAK? SHE AGED OUT LAST YEAR AGO, BLESS HER HEART.

BEST SEAMSTRESS I EVER MET-- SEWED ALL HER OWN GOWNS.
BUT YOU COULD SEE IN HER EYES THAT SHE'D RATHER BE ANYWHERE BUT HERE.
IS THAT TEAK AS IN ***DESIGNED BY TEAK?***

YES, MA'AM. THAT'S HER MOMMA'S SHOP.

IT'S THAT LITTLE PLACE OFF MURRAY STREET. YOU KNOW THE ONE, RIGHT?
VROOOOM

I THINK SO.
GREAT! THE RIDE-ALONG'S BEEN FUN, BUT COULD YOU DROP ME AT WORK? DON'T WANNA MISS MY SHIFT!
SURE, DIANE.

SMEK

Um, GOLDIE? I WAS THINKING...
IT MIGHT BE THE TIME TO LOOP IN THE FBI.

C'MON, WALT. DESIGNED BY TEAK IS ON THE WAY BACK TO CROSSED PALMS. WHAT'LL IT HURT IF WE SWING BY?
siiigh

VRRRRRM

Hmm. NO SIGN OF CHERYL'S CAR.
Designed BY Teaks

ding ding
MAY I HELP YOU?

IS MILLIE HERE? WE'RE OLD FRIENDS FROM THE *CIRCUIT*, AND--
SHE'S GONE, DOLL. RAN OFF MONTHS AGO.

SHE RAN AWAY?!
A JOB AT MOMMA'S SWIM SHOP AIN'T GOOD ENOUGH FOR MILLICENT. BUT SHE'S EIGHTEEN; SHE CAN DO WHAT SHE LIKES.

IN MY EXPERIENCE, WHEN A GIRL SETS HER MIND TO SOMETHING, THERE'S NO STOPPING HER.

BAHAHAHAHAHAHA!

Um, MILLIE *BORROWED* SOMETHING FROM ME, AND I WAS HOPING...

CHECK HER ROOM, IF YOU LIKE. IT'S THIS WAY.

WHAT IS IT YOU'RE LOOKING FOR?
Oh--A BOOK.

A BOOK? MILLIE WAS A MAGAZINE KINDA GIRL.
SIXTEEN

SHE DIDN'T LIKE SCIENCE, OR ASTRONOMY, OR...?

HEAVENS, NO! GENTLEMEN FIND BRAINY GIRLS OFF-PUTTING. DON'T YOU AGREE, MR...?
Er--TOOEY. MR. TOOEY. AND I CAN'T, ah, SAY THAT I DO.

NO? FASCINATING.
ANY SIGN OF THAT BOOK, GOLDIE? 'CAUSE WE'D BETTER GET GOING.

GOLDIE...?

GAAASP

WHEW. THOUGHT I WAS GONNA DROWN IN TULLE.
YEAH, WE CAN GO.

THANKS FOR YOUR TIME, MS. TEAK. YOUR SWIMSUITS ARE BEAUTIFUL.
AREN'T THEY? ***MILLIE*** DIDN'T THINK SO.

SHE INSISTED ON WEARING THOSE CHEAP ***JOYTEX*** SUITS OFF THE RACK. I CAN'T EVEN ***TOUCH*** THEM--THE FABRIC GIVES ME ***HIVES.***

!!

BE RIGHT BACK--

IF JOYTEX SWIMSUITS GIVE MS. TEAK HIVES--

THAT'S WHERE MILLIE WOULD KEEP HER SECRETS.

A-HA!

JOYTEX GOES·TO SPACE
Swimwear brand lands contract to manufacture NASA space suits.

Have You Ever Wanted
to live in outer space? Seeking like-minded voyagers.
CALL BOX #772

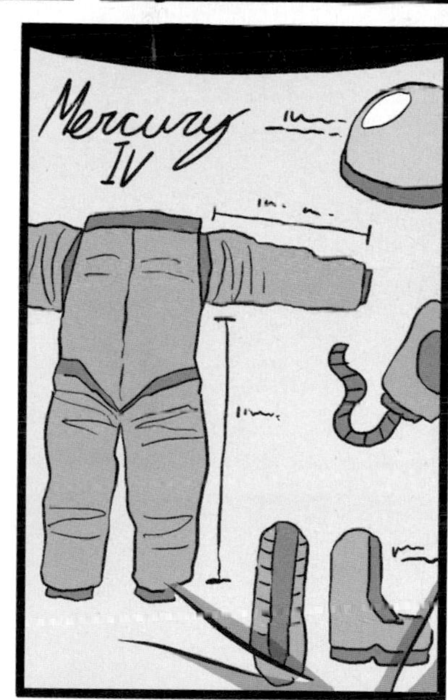
Mercury IV

MILLIE DIDN'T WANT TO MAKE SWIMSUITS; SHE WANTED TO MAKE SPACESUITS.

THANKS, MS. TEAK! C'MON, WALTER!
What took you?! I was in peril!
DON'T BE A STRANGER, WALTER!

Hmm. A NEWSPAPER AD? THAT'S NO HELP. THEY EXPIRE AFTER A WEEK.

MAYBE IF WE CALL THE PAPER--
NOPE. THEY DON'T KEEP RECORDS. TRUST ME, I HAVE PERSONAL EXPERIENCE WITH THE LONELY HEARTS SECTION.

SO THAT'S IT. DEAD END.

GUESS THE FBI CAN TAKE IT FROM HERE.

IF SOMEONE DOESN'T FIND CHERYL SOON, I'LL BE THE FIRST GIRL WHO MADE HER FRIEND MAD ENOUGH TO LEAVE THE PLANET.
STOP

CHERYL'S NOT LEAVING THE PLANET, AND NEITHER IS MILLIE.
DUNNO, WALT. A GREAT MAN ONCE SAID, "WHEN A GIRL SETS HER MIND TO SOMETHING, THERE'S NO STOPPING HER."

Pfft. **THINK,** GOLDIE. YOU FOUND MILLIE ON THE BEACH.
YEAH, AND?

AND SHE GREW UP IN A **SWIM SHOP.**
AND A SPACE SUIT'S ALMOST A **SCUBA** SUIT, RIGHT?

SO YOU'RE SAYING MILLIE...
MILLIE DIDN'T COME **DOWN** FROM THE SKY.

SHE CAME UP FROM UNDERWATER.

chapter SEVEN

issue seven cover by **Brittney Williams**

MILLIE DIDN'T COME DOWN FROM THE SKY, GOLDIE.
SHE CAME UP FROM UNDERWATER.
THAT'S IT, WALTER!

THAT'S IT! THAT'S WHY SHE COULDN'T REMEMBER WHO SHE WAS!
Huh? EXPLAIN.

MY MOM GOT HER SCUBA CERTIFICATION WHEN I WAS LITTLE, AND I HELPED HER STUDY.
SHE HAD TO MEMORIZE THESE CHARTS FOR HOW FAST YOU CAN SURFACE. DIVE TABLES.

IF YOU COME UP TOO FAST, YOU GET BUBBLES ALL INSIDE YOUR BODY.
Ugh. SOUNDS PAINFUL.

IT IS. AND YOU KNOW WHAT ANOTHER SYMPTOM IS?
AMNESIA.
Oh. Oh.

YEAH. MILLIE HAD THE BENDS.

GOLDIE, I THINK IT'S TIME--
TO TELL THE FBI? I KNOW.

I WONDER WHAT AGENT LADNER'S GONNA SAY.

CROSSED PALMS RESORT.
THIS IS INCREDIBLE, WALTER.

INCREDIBLE THAT YOU WERE ABLE TO STUMBLE ONTO SO MANY CLUES.

HOPE WE DIDN'T, uh, IMPEDE YOUR INVESTIGATION.

TO BE EXPECTED, TOOEY. YOU WERE ALWAYS TROUBLE-- EVEN IN HIGH SCHOOL.
TROUBLE? WALTER?

HE TELL YA HOW WE MET?

I BUSTED HIM SELLING ANSWERS TO ALGEBRA TESTS.
Aw, LAYLA, THERE'S NO NEED TO--

WHAT?! WALTER WAS A J.D.?!*
*Juvenile delinquent.

Aw, COME ON! I'VE BEEN REFORMED SINCE SOPHOMORE YEAR!
STILL, I THINK I'D BETTER KEEP A CLOSER EYE ON YOU.

ME! GOLDIE'S THE ONE WHO--

Huh? WHERE'D SHE GO?

NOT TO WORRY-- SHE'S A BIG GIRL.

"SHE CAN TAKE CARE OF HERSELF."

NOW THAT THE LOVEBIRDS ARE INVESTIGATING EACH OTHER, I CAN GET ON WITH MY OWN INVESTIGATION.

MERMAID CLUB

SHE'S IN THE DRESSING ROOM.
THANKS, LIZZIE!

MOM?

GOLDIE! WHAT ARE YOU DOING HERE?
XOX

I NEED SOME AQUATIC ADVICE.
YOU *DO*?

Oh, SWEETIE, YOU'LL MAKE AN ***ADORABLE*** MERMAID! HAVE YOU PICKED A COLOR FOR YOUR TAIL?
Um-- SORRY TO BURST YOUR ***BUBBLE,*** BUT--

I KNOW WHAT THIS IS. IT'S A DETECTIVE THING.

LIZZIE! TWO SHIRLEY TEMPLES, EXTRA CHERRIES.

...SO I THINK MILLIE MIGHT BE TAKING CHERYL BACK WHERE SHE CAME FROM. AND IF SHE CAME FROM THE **OCEAN,** THEY'LL NEED SCUBA GEAR.

AND YOU NEED SOMEONE WHO KNOWS THE DIVING WORLD. AN INSIDER.
YEAH.

BAD NEWS, KID. A MERMAID'S HELP AIN'T FREE.

I'LL WASH THE DISHES FOR A MONTH.

AND?

AND I'LL RE-CAULK THE BATHTUB.

AND WE'RE SIGNING UP FOR MER-FAMILY DAY.

WHAT?! BUT--

I'M TIRED OF CYNTHIA AND HER SON WINNING EVERY YEAR WITH THE SAME SOGGY ROUTINE.

ORANGE, OKAY?

I WANT MY TAIL TO BE ORANGE.

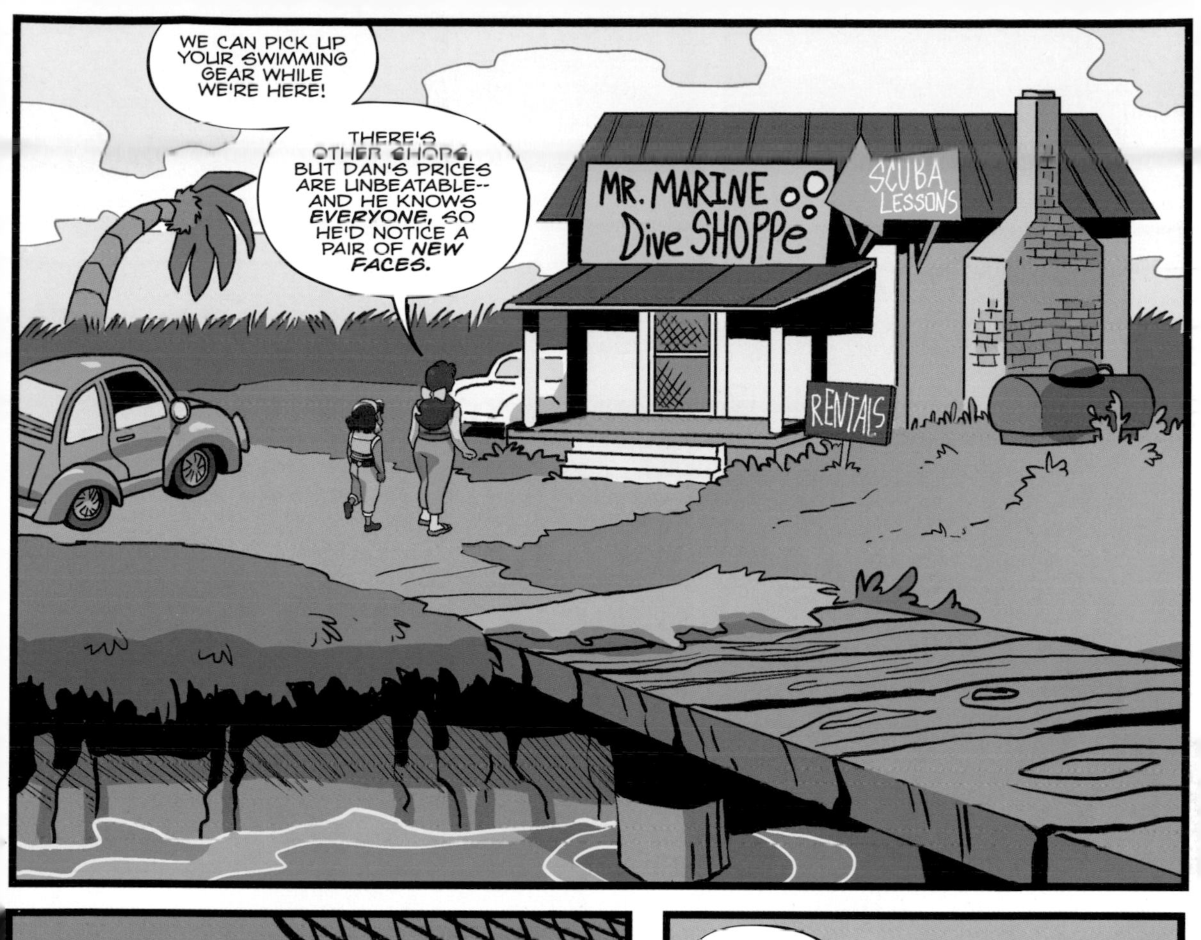
WE CAN PICK UP YOUR SWIMMING GEAR WHILE WE'RE HERE!
THERE'S OTHER SHOPS, BUT DAN'S PRICES ARE UNBEATABLE-- AND HE KNOWS *EVERYONE*, SO HE'D NOTICE A PAIR OF *NEW FACES*.
MR. MARINE Dive SHOPPE
SCUBA LESSONS
RENTALS

HEY, DANNY! HOW YA BEEN?

SORRY, BUT... HAVE WE MET?

SILLY! YOU ALMOST GOT ME.

MY APOLOGIES, MISS. I CAN SEE YOU AIN'T THE KINDA WOMAN A FELLA FORGETS.
BUT I HAD A LITTLE ACCIDENT WITH AN EXPLODING OXYGEN TANK A FEW WEEKS AGO, AN' I'VE BEEN KINDA ABSENTMINDED SINCE.
WOW. DIVING'S TERRIBLE FOR YOUR MEMORY.

IF YOU DON'T REMEMBER ME, I DON'T SUPPOSE YOU'D REMEMBER A PAIR OF YOUNG LADIES WHO STOPPED BY TODAY OR YESTERDAY?

I'D HAFTA CHECK MY RECORDS. BUT THEY'RE CONFIDENTIAL, I'M AFRAID

THAT'S ALL RIGHT. WHY DON'T YOU COME OVER HERE AND SHOW ME THE FINS?
SURE THING!

WE'LL BE RIGHT BACK, GOLDIE.
wink

SHE WANTS ME TO DO SOMETHING-- BUT WHAT?

THAT'S IT! SHE WANTS ME TO CHECK THE

WHAT'S THE DIFFERENCE BETWEEN AN PROPEL X90 AND A SHARKSPEED 10?
WELL, SEE THIS CENTER CHANNEL ON THE SHARKSPEED?

THAT'S THEIR SIGNATURE ELEMENT, AND IF YOU ASK *ME*--WHICH YOU ARE--
AND THANK GOODNESS YOUR TECHNICAL EXPERTISE WASN'T HARMED IN THE ACCIDENT!
RATS. NO TIME TO PICK THE LOCK.

BUT... THE RECEIPT PAD? Hm...

...BUT WITH THE X90, YOU WON'T HAVE TO SACRIFICE **FLEXIBILITY** FOR--
SORRY TO CUT THIS SHORT, MOM, BUT WE GOTTA GO.

THAT WAS EASY!
FOR **YOU**, MAYBE. *Ugh.*
SO THEY WERE HERE?

YUP!

SEE?
MR. MARINE
DIVE SHOPPE
NAME
DATE
DESCRIPTION
Price
FINS
MASK
SNORKEL

Huh. INTERESTING. BASED ON THE GEAR THEY BOUGHT, I HAVE A HUNCH THEY'RE HEADING TO THE STRAITS.
THE WHAT?

HERE-- I'LL SHOW YOU.

THE FLORIDA STRAITS LIE ALONGSIDE THE FLORIDA PENINSULA AND CURL UNDERNEATH THE KEYS--LIKE A GREAT BIG J.
THINK OF THEM AS A LONG, NARROW UNDERWATER VALLEY.
OKAY. BUT WHY WOULD MILLIE GO THERE?

THERE ARE RUMORS ABOUT A SECRET MILITARY BASE HIDDEN THERE, BUILT BY THE U.S. NAVY DURING WORLD WAR II IN ORDER TO MONITOR ENEMY SUBS, AND ABANDONED AFTER THE ARMISTICE.
BUT LEMME GUESS-- NO ONE'S EVER FOUND IT.

SUNSHINE OIL & GAS SPENT THE LAST TWO YEARS DRILLING IN THE STRAITS.
IF THERE WAS A BASE TO FIND, THEY'D HAVE BEEN THE ONES TO DO IT--AND I'D HAVE HEARD ALL ABOUT IT.

WE GOT PLENTY OF SUNSHINE'S DIVERS AT THE MERMAID CLUB.
DID YOU DATE ANY OF 'EM?

ONE. THIS FELLOW, JACK.
NOT SURE HOW HE MANAGED TO DIVE WHEN HE WAS SO FULL OF HOT AIR.

AND HE WAS TOO SHORT FOR ME. YOU KNOW HOW I LOVE MY HEELS.

LUCKY FOR ME, SUNSHINE DIDN'T STRIKE OIL AND MOVED THEIR OPERATION TO THE GULF OF MEXICO, AND HE WENT, TOO.

IF SUNSHINE COULDN'T FIND OIL, MAYBE THE BASE IS THERE, AND THEY COULDN'T FIND IT, EITHER.
MAYBE NOT.

HOW SHORT WAS HE?
MY HEIGHT. 5'10".

I'M EVEN 5'10", THE IDEAL ASTRONAUT HEIGHT!

Huh.

SYLVIE & GOLDIE'S APARTMENT.
Oh, WOULD YOU--I'M COMING!
rrringg

WHAT? NOW? I'M WITH MY DAUGHTER, JEMMA! I TOLD YOU, I--

OKAY, FINE. BUT THIS IS THE LAST TIME.

AND YOU HAVE TO COVER FOR ME ON THE...
THE 16th. I HAVE A DATE.

SORRY, HONEY.
click

I'M HEADING BACK OUT, BUT WE'LL START PLANNING OUR MERMAID ROUTINE TOMORROW.
WE CAN PUT IT OFF EVEN LONGER IF THAT'D HELP. LIKE, FOREVER.

CHEEKY.

Y.P. FLORIDA

IF MOM WRITES DOWN ALL HER DATES, MAYBE SHE WROTE DOWN HER ONE WITH--
fwip

FLASH! THERE HE IS!

fwip fwip fwip
FLORIDA
Y.P. FLORIDA

IF SUNSHINE OIL & GAS MOVED TO THE GULF OF MEXICO, HOW COME FIDLER'S STILL IN THE PHONE BOOK?

NO LIGHTS.

jiggle
CLICK

GHOST FURNITURE. SPOOKY.

HE MUST NOT BE LIVING HERE.

THE BED'S BEEN SLEPT IN, RECENTLY-ISH.

Huh?

HIS SUNSHINE OIL & GAS SCHEDULE.
MAN! MY VALET SHIFTS FEEL ENDLESS, BUT AT LEAST THEY DON'T LAST FIFTEEN DAYS.

IF HE LIVES HERE BETWEEN SHIFTS, HE WON'T BE BACK 'TIL TOMORROW.

MAYBE I'LL COME TALK TO HIM THEN.

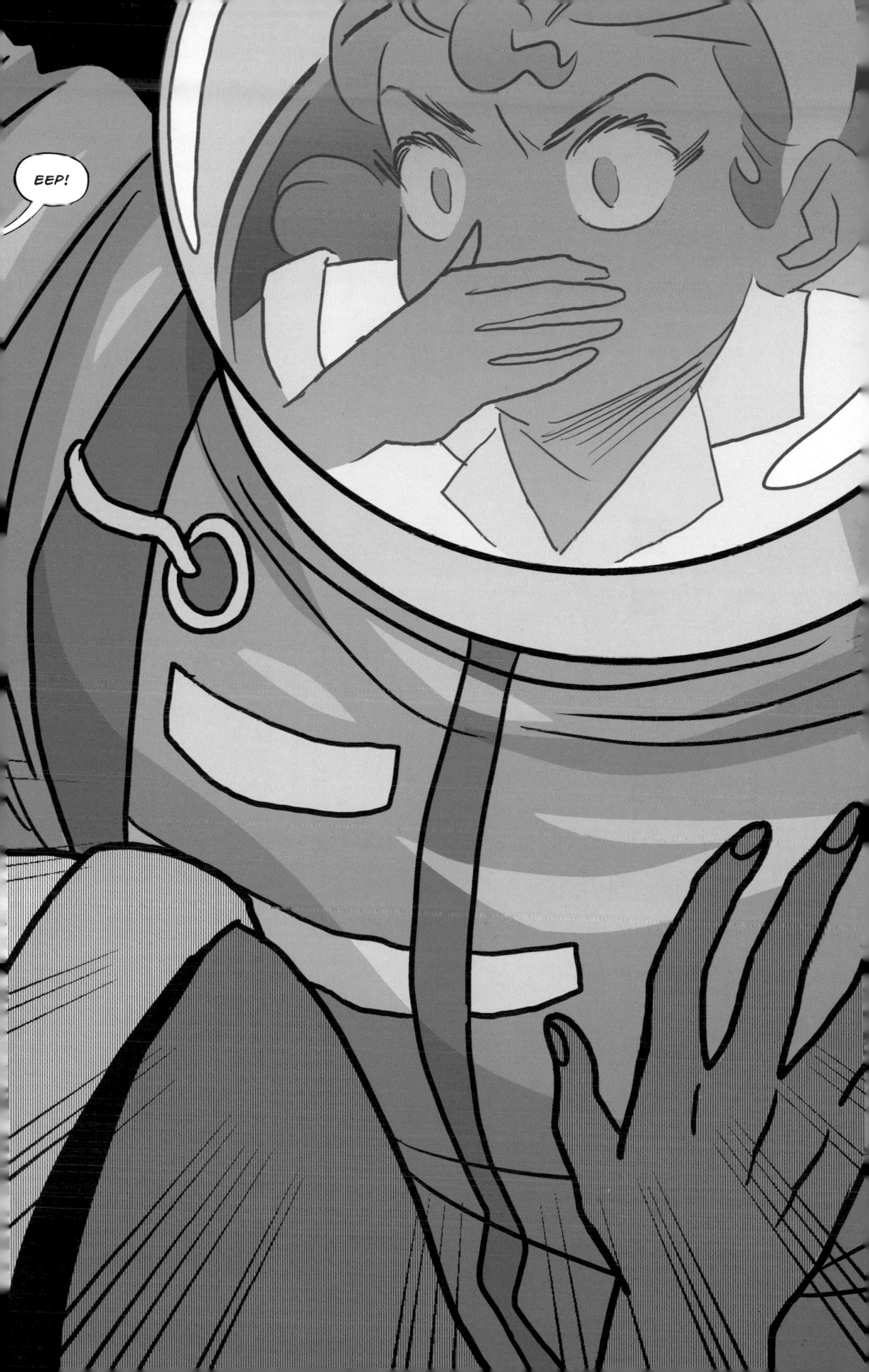
EEP!

Whew...
IT'S OKAY...
JUST AN EMPTY SPACE SUIT.

IT MUST BE ANOTHER OF **MILLIE'S.** AND THIS ONE'S DESIGNED FOR UNDERWATER, TOO.

NAS
WHOA.

NASA

"DEAR MR. FIDLER, WE REGRET TO INFORM YOU THAT, AFTER MUCH DELIBERATION, YOUR APPLICATION TO THE ASTRONAUT PROGRAM HAS BEEN **REJECTED.**"

FLORIDA
ST. PASCAL
IF HE CAN'T GO TO SPACE, MAYBE A **SECRET OCEAN BASE** IS THE NEXT BEST THING.

AND SO...
I WAS TRYING ,NOT TO "BORROW" ANY VEHICLES, BUT DOES A BOAT REALLY COUNT?
VRRRRRRRRRR

I'M SORRY, CHERYL. I'M SORRY I MADE YOU FEEL LIKE YOU WEREN'T **GOOD ENOUGH**.

YOU CAN'T GIVE UP YOUR DREAM FOR THE NEXT BEST THING.
VRRRRR

I WON'T LET YOU.

MEANWHILE, DEEP IN THE FLORIDA STRAITS...
"JUST HANG ON. I'LL BE THERE SOON."

GULF OF MEXICO
FLORIDA
STRAITS
OF
FLORIDA

chapter

EIGHT

issue eight cover by **Kat Leyh**

REALLY? I'M REALLY DOING THIS?

I'M SCARED.
I'M NOT USED TO BEING SCARED.

YOU'D DO THIS FOR ME, RIGHT, CHERYL? DIANE SAID TO PUT MYSELF IN YOUR SHOES.

YOU WOULD.
I KNOW YOU WOULD.

"YOU COME THROUGH FOR ME NO MATTER WHAT DUMB STUFF I PULL.
"I'M THE ONE FLOATING AWAY, AND YOU'RE THE ANCHOR. I'M THE JOKER, AND YOU'RE THE QUEEN.
"I NEVER THOUGHT YOU COULD BE INSECURE. I'M SO SORRY I HURT YOU.
"YOU KEPT ME GROUNDED SO MANY TIMES, CHERYL-- NOW I'M GOING TO LIFT YOU BACK UP WHERE YOU BELONG.
"JUST HANG ON. I'LL BE THERE SOON."

THERE!

THE BASE--IT'S REAL!

kick
kick kick
GOTTA-- GO-- FASTER!

Whew NEED A BREATHER. SHOULDA MADE AN EFFORT WHEN CHER TOOK ME JOGGING.

kickkickkickkick
RRRGH!
ALMOST-- THERE--

MADE IT!

NOW, WHAT'S THE WAY IN?

Gasp

CHERYL! AND THAT'S MILLIE!

?
YIPES! THAT WAS CLOSE.

Huh?

BINGO! THIS MUST BE THE ENTRANCE!

THE AIRLOCK.

GACK!
AIEEE!
grab

NOW, ALEC!
NNNGH--
-KOFF-
-KOFF-
-KOFF-
ARE YOU OUT OF YOUR MIND?
KOFF?

YOU RUINED NASA FOR ME--NOW YOU WANT TO RUIN THIS, TOO?
I JUST WANTED TO... TO...

TO BE AN ASTRONAUT?

NO! IT'S MY DREAM, NOT HERS!

THAT'S WHY I'M HERE, CHERYL! BECAUSE THIS ISN'T YOUR DREAM!

YOU'RE RIGHT. IT'S NOT.

IT'S SOMETHING BETTER.

THE COMMONS.
PROJECT DEEPSTAR WAS CONCEIVED AS A TRAINING PROGRAM FOR THOSE TRULY **COMMITTED** COSMONAUTS WHO FEEL NASA'S APPROACH IS TOO, *ah,* ***LACKADAISICAL.***
THIS IS THE COMMON AREA, WHERE WE PLAY GAMES.
Game, *she means. Chess is all we have.*

THE DORMS.
DEEPSTAR COSMONAUTS LIVE AND TRAIN 24/7 IN THE INHOSPITABLE DEPTHS OF THE OCEAN.

THE KITCHEN.
WHEN P.D. COMPLETES HIS ROCKET, WE'LL BE PREPARED FOR THE CHALLENGES OF SPACE IN A WAY NASA'S PART-TIMERS NEVER WILL.
I thought I hated vegetables, but now? I could eat a fresh head of lettuce like it was an ***apple.***
RICE
PeaNut Butter
POTABLE WATER

SO, WHO'S "P.D."?
THE PROGRAM DIRECTOR.

YOU MEAN JACK? JACK FIDLER?

DON'T ACT FAMILIAR! HE'S A GREAT MAN, AND HE DESERVES OUR RESPECT.
YEAH? IF HE'S SO GREAT, HOW COME YOU WASHED UP ON THE BEACH OUTSIDE CROSSED PALMS?

THAT WAS OUR MISTAKE, NOT HIS. WE FAILED.
NO, ALEC--YOU FAILED.

THE STOREROOM.
WHAT HAPPENED WAS, A FEW DAYS AGO, THE STOREROOM SPRANG A LEAK.

"LUCKILY, P.D. LEFT US EPOXY FOR REPAIRS--

"BUT ALEC CAME UNGLUED AND MIXED IT WRONG."
Uh-oh. HOW MUCH HARDENER DID YOU ADD?!
ALL OF IT? I DON'T KNOW! I PANICKED!

"SOMEONE HAD TO GO TO TOPSIDE AND BUY MORE, BUT WE ONLY HAD ONE SPACE SUIT.
"ONE CHANCE AT SURVIVAL.

"SO, I WENT.

"BUT I RAN INTO SOME TROUBLE. THERE WASN'T TIME FOR ANY STOPS.
"THERE WOULDN'T BE SHARKS IF I WAS IN SPACE!"

IF CHERYL HADN'T FOUND ME--IF IT HAD BEEN ANYONE BUT A TRUE-BLUE PAGEANT GIRL--
ACTUALLY, MILLIE...

GOLDIE AND I FOUND YOU TOGETHER.

SO? SHE DIDN'T COME BACK TO HELP ME. YOU DID. IF YOU HADN'T, I'D STILL BE UP THERE, AND ALEC WOULD BE STANDING ON A BOX, SUCKING AIR OFF THE CEILING.

HOLD ON. BACK IT UP. ONE SPACE SUIT? THAT'S INSANE!
TWO WOULD MAKE IT TOO EASY.

IT WOULDN'T PROPERLY SIMULATE THE ISOLATION AND PERIL OF A SPACE STATION.
THAT'S WHY P.D. FOUNDED PROJECT DEEPSTAR. HE NEVER FELT CHALLENGED BY NASA.

HE DIDN'T FEEL CHALLENGED?

HAHAHA! YOU'RE DARN RIGHT HE DIDN'T!
WHAT'S THE DEAL?! WHY ARE YOU LAUGHING?

P.D. WASN'T CHALLENGED BY NASA BECAUSE, WHEN HE APPLIED TO THEIR SPACE PROGRAM, HE WAS REJECTED!
HE'S NOT AN ASTRONAUT! HE'S NOT EVEN A SCIENTIST!
HE'S A DELUSIONAL CREEP WHO WORKS AS A DIVER FOR SUNSHINE OIL & GAS.
AND I'VE BEEN TO HIS HOUSE, AND THERE'S NO ROCKET.

SHUT UP! IT'S NOT TRUE! HE'S BEEN BUILDING IT FOR MONTHS!

DON'T TELL HER TO SHUT UP!
BUT SHE'S LYING! SHE'S ***LYING!***

SHE'S MY ***BEST FRIEND*** AND SHE CAME ***ALL THIS WAY*** TO GET RIGHT WITH ME!

COME ON, MILLIE. IT'S LOOKING-GLASS TIME.
DID YOU WIN ALL THOSE BEAUTY PAGEANTS AND SPEND ALL THOSE YEARS UNDER YOUR MOTHER'S THUMB SO A ***CON MAN*** COULD TRAP YOU IN AN UNDERWATER ***BOX?***

YOU'RE ALL STAKING YOUR LIVES ON THE DREAM OF A CLOD WHO COULDN'T HANDLE REJECTION.
THIS PLACE IS A MESS AND A HALF. IF YOU DON'T GET OUT OF HERE, YOU'RE GONNA ***DIE.***

THUNK
Eep!

YOU'VE ***CONTAMINATED*** THE BASE.
P.D.!

WHAT WERE YOU THINKING, BRINGING *ALIEN LIFE FORMS* ON BOARD?!

P.D., PLEASE DON'T BE ANGRY! THEY'RE NOT ALIENS! THEY'RE JUST GIRLS.
WE ALMOST *DIED,* AND THEY HELPED US!

IN SPACE, THERE'S NO SUCH THING AS HELP. IN SPACE, YOU'D BE DEAD ALREADY.
KRAK
UNGH!

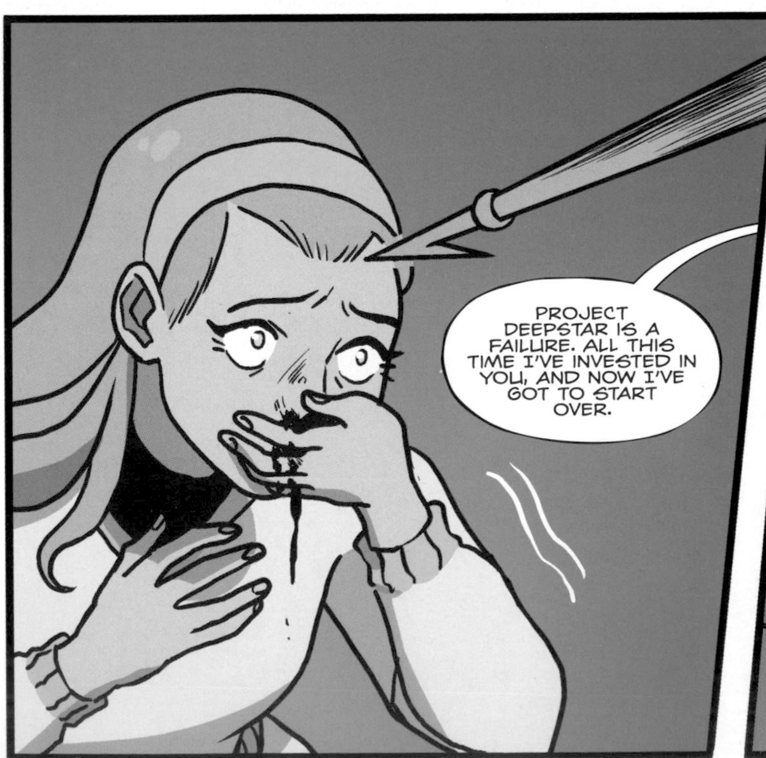
PROJECT DEEPSTAR IS A FAILURE. ALL THIS TIME I'VE INVESTED IN YOU, AND NOW I'VE GOT TO START OVER.

KRRRRK

NO!
HURK!
PFOW
SHRIEK!
NOW YOU'VE DONE IT.

C'MON! STEP ON IT! *MOVE!*
I'LL HOLD HIM! DON'T--DON'T WAIT FOR ME!
WHUD

Ungh...

JEEZ, HOW MANY HARPOONS DOES THAT THING HOLD?!
PFOW PFOW PFOW
C'MON! THIS WAY!
SLAM
WE'LL BE SAFE HERE 'TIL I COME UP WITH A PLAN.
No... Not safe.
No locks.
AAAH!

THINK FAST, GOLDIE.
THINK.
THINK!

Ah-HA!
?!

YAAAA!
SMOOOSH
ARGH!

KLAAANG
GOOD ARM, CHER!
YEP. NOT MUCH TO DO DOWN HERE BUT PUSH-UPS.

SOON...
Unh... AM I DEAD?
NO, BUDDY. NOT *YET.*

Oh **NO!** I FORGOT-- WE'RE SHORT A SUIT!
I'VE BEEN CHEWING ON THAT SINCE I GOT HERE. I HAVE A PLAN.

MILLIE, YOU TAKE THE SPACE SUIT. WE DON'T WANT YOUR NOSEBLEED ATTRACTING SHARKS.

ALEC, YOU TAKE A WHOLE SUIT. YOU'RE AN ***ANXIOUS*** GUY-- YOU'LL NEED ALL THE AIR YOU CAN GET.

WHAT ABOUT *US?*
WE'RE GONNA SHARE.

WILL THAT WORK?!
IT WORKED FOR ASTRONAUTS SILK AND HAMAKER WHEN THEIR SHIP SUFFERED A LEAK IN ORBIT.
AS LONG AS WE STAY ***CALM--***

"WE'LL BE
JUST FINE."

HUH?!

MOM?!

AND AGENT LADNER!

AND... WALTER CAN SCUBA DIVE?!
MAN! EVERYONE'S FULL OF SURPRISES.

MAYBE I AM, TOO. MAYBE I'LL TAKE UP JOGGING AFTER ALL. THAT'D BLOW THEIR MINDS!

THAT'S BUNK, GOLDIE VANCE, AND YOU KNOW IT.
Huh?! YOU CAN READ MY THOUGHTS?!

THAT, OR WE'RE LOW ON OXYGEN.
HANG IN THERE, BESTIE--WE'RE ALMOST THERE!

krack
YEOWCH!

I'M SORRY, MISS. YOUR NOSE WILL HEAL UP FINE, BUT YOU'LL ALWAYS HAVE A *BUMP.*
GOOD. I DIDN'T LIKE BEING PERFECT, ANYWAY.

HEY, CHER... GOT ANY PLANS NEXT WEEKEND?
YOU WANNA DO SOMETHING?

WITH *YOU? NAH.* I WAS HOPING I COULD BORROW YOUR CAR.
...

KIDDING! JUST KIDDING!
Uh-huh. SEE YOU TOMORROW, GOLDIE.

Um--YOU CAN'T STILL READ MY MIND, RIGHT? RIGHT, CHERYL?
Heh heh.

CHERYL?
CHER?
THE END

CASE STUDY

from script to page

ISSUE FIVE: PAGE ONE

PANEL ONE: A large panel. Cheryl is running along the beach, moving left to right, the ocean sunrise behind her. It's all very *Chariots of Fire*. She looks beautiful and serene.

CAPTION: St. Pascal, Florida

CAPTION: 5:45 AM

PANEL TWO: A side view of Cheryl's sneaker-clad feet as she runs across the packed sand, hardly leaving any footprints. In the background, the ocean is lapping at the beach.

SFX: Paff

PANEL THREE: Close on Cheryl. A drop or two of sweat on her brow; a tiny puff of breath at her lips.

SFX: Huff

PANEL FOUR: Close on Cheryl, eyes widening.

CHERYL: GASP!

ISSUE FIVE: PAGE TWO

PANEL ONE: Goldie's flopped down on the sand, propped halfway up on the side of a sand dune, fast asleep and snoring. Cheryl has stopped, hands on her hips, to glare down at her friend.

GOLDIE: Z z z z . . .

CHERYL: Goldie!

PANEL TWO: Goldie startles awake, sitting upright in a hurry. She's totally out of it.

GOLDIE: Wh-wha's wrong, Cheryl?!

CHERYL: When I said go at your own pace, I didn't mean go to sleep!

PANEL THREE: Goldie pretends to stretch. She's so full of it and so adorable.

GOLDIE: I wasn't asleep! I was -- I was *stretching*. Gotta stay limber.

CHERYL: Ugh. At this rate you'll never pass the physical!

PANEL FOUR: Cheryl helps pull Goldie up off the sand.

GOLDIE: We aren't all destined to be astronauts like *you*.

CHERYL: I can't believe you'd trade all of outer space for another hour of sleep! What about science? What about the mysteries of the cosmos?

PANEL FIVE: Goldie and Cheryl are walking around the edge of a dune which has blocked their view down the rest of the beach.

CHERYL: What about *drag-racing* on the moon?

PANEL SIX: Close on Cheryl and Goldie. Cheryl's head is turned toward Goldie. Goldie's staring straight ahead, wide-eyed with concern.

CHERYL: Moon gravity is a *sixth* of what it is on Earth, so I bet there's all *kinds* of cool tricks you could --

GOLDIE: Hey, Cher? Are you sure you woke me up?

ISSUE FIVE: PAGE THREE

PANEL ONE: Large panel. Goldie and Cheryl have stopped in their tracks. Lying face-down on the beach in front of them is an astronaut in a space suit. The astronaut's helmet is on, and its mirror surface obscures the person inside. The suit should look just like a Mercury IV space suit except for one thing: there are no NASA logos anywhere on it.

Important: In the background of this panel we should see the back of Crossed Palms; this is setting something up for a later scene.

GOLDIE: Or am I dreaming?

CHERYL: Unreal!

OR AM I DREAMING?
UNREAL!

WRITTEN BY **PAMELA RIBON**
ILLUSTRATED BY **VERONICA FISH**
COLORS BY **BRITTNEY PEER**
LETTERS BY **JIM CAMPBELL**

In roller derby you take your hits, get back up, and learn how to be a better jammer, a better blocker, a better lover, and a better friend. Derby can heal your heart...but it might break a bone or two in the process.

***SLAM!* Vol. 1 Softcover • $14.99 • ISBN: 978-1-68415-004-5**

SCRAPES DRESSING ROOM 6:30 PM.
BOUT DAY!
SKATE FAST
SKATE HARD
TURN LEFT!
Get LOW
HIT SOMEBODY
PIZZA 4 CLOSERS
Itinerary
5:30 Get here!
6:00 Where the F R U?!
7:00 WARM UPS
7:30 Team Meet
7:45 Get on the track!
8:00 FIRST WHISTLE!
ROCKEM SHOCKEM 55
PATTY NUKES 90
POWER PROTEIN
IGLOO
APRIL 4th 8PM
EAST SIDE ROLLER GIRLS
ROOKIE RUMBLE!
SCARS VS SCRAPES

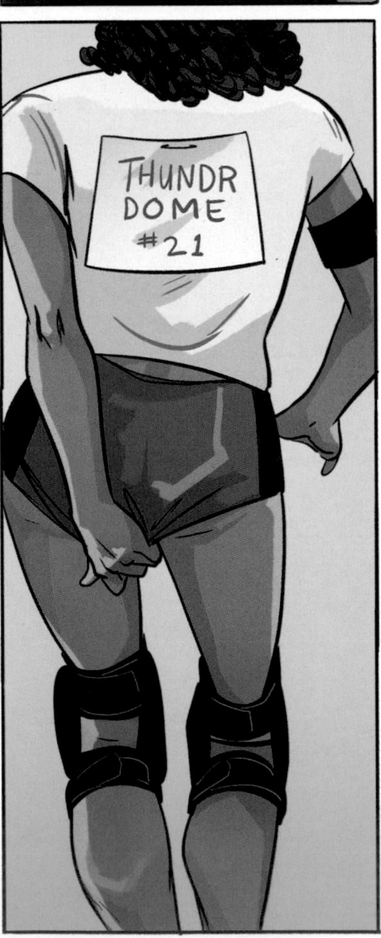
THUNDR
DOME
#21

I WISH WE'D JUST GET STARTED ALREADY. I'M SO NERVOUS.
I'VE POOPED *SIX* *TIMES.*
TAP TAP

I CAN'T DO IT.
MOISIE. YOU CAN. YOU HAVE TO. YOU *WILL.*
LOOK, THE FATE OF THIS GAME IS ALREADY DETERMINED. GO FIND OUT WHAT IT IS.
Don't call me
23-304-2979
THAT'S A *HORRIBLE* PHILOSOPHY.
YOU GOT THROUGH THE PAST YEAR. YOU CAN GET THROUGH THE NEXT TWO HOURS.
I CAN'T BELIEVE I HAVEN'T KNOWN YOU ALL THAT TIME, JEN.

THIS IS JENNIFER CHU.
AKA: KNOCKOUT.
AKA: YOUR NEXT DERBY CRUSH.
A.D.
AFTER DERBY
MARKER doodles
Jammer extraordinaire
FEARLESS
Doesn't have a tattoo
(she's a rare unicorn!)
Good at pep talks
Always roots for the underdog
P.D.
PRE-DERBY
(aka 6 months ago)
BIG BRAIN
Getting a masters in geology
(a little obsessed with earthquakes)
(because they are coming)
(like, science says so.)
Close with her parents
SHE NEEDED DERBY AS MUCH AS DERBY NEEDED HER.

THIS IS MAISIE HUFF.
AKA: TTHINKA CAN
YOUR NEW BEST FRIEND.
P.D.
(Pre-Derby)
▷ Recently DUMPED!
▷ Too skinny from a diet consisting of tears and fury!
▷ Still sleeps on his side of the bed!
▷ Pathetic and KNOWS IT!
A.D.
(After-Derby)
Starting to remember that life DOESN'T suck!
▷ Sometimes changes out of her pajamas!
▷ Intentionally eating to gain weight so people stop calling her hips "KNIFE BONES"
▷ Learning how to get back up after a FALL...
EAST SIDE ROLLER GIRLS
BUT FIRST SHE HAD TO...
TO BE CONTINUED IN SLAM! VOLUME ONE!